Puff
in the Land
of the Living Lies

by Romeo Muller

Illustrations by Fred Wolf and Chuck Swenson
Based on the TV special

TROLL ASSOCIATES

Puff in the Land of the Living Lies
is an original publication of Troll Books.
This work has never before appeared in book form.

"Puff (The Magic Dragon)"
Words by Peter Yarrow and Leonard Lipton.
Copyright © 1979 by PePaMar Music Corp.
"What the World Can Be"
Words and Music by Peter Yarrow.
Copyright © 1980 by Silver Dawn Music (ASCAP).
"The Walls Come Tumblin' Down"
Words and Music by Peter Yarrow.
Copyright © 1980 by Silver Dawn Music (ASCAP).

Illustrations by Fred Wolf and Chuck Swenson
based on the TV special.

Troll Books

A division of Troll Associates
Mahwah, New Jersey 07430.
Copyright © 1982 by The My Company.
Published by arrangement with The My Company.
Library of Congress Catalog Card Number: 82-51113
ISBN: 0-89375-868-X

For information address
Robert Lewis Rosen Associates
7 West 51 Street
New York, New York 10019.

First Troll Printing, January, 1984

Printed in the United States of America

This book is dedicated to
Bob Rosen and Kevin Hunter

CONTENTS

SONGS

CHAPTER ONE

Sandy Was Unique

*Puff the magic dragon
Lived by the sea
And frolicked in the autumn mist
In a land called Honah Lee.*

The alarm clock rang loudly. "Lunch time!" shouted Puff, settling himself beneath his favorite tree. He tucked the alarm clock back into his pocket and made a magic gesture. A fully set kitchen table appeared in a puff of smoke. He looked at the

7

meal spread before him. There were textbooks and notepads and pencils and erasers.

"Ah, homework! My favorite food!" cried the ravenous dragon, picking up a volume in one hand and a ketchup bottle in the other. "An arithmetic book! Yummy! Ketchup goes well with higher mathematics. Then a bite of geography with mustard. And I'll wash it all down with some geometry juice."

WAIT! HOLD IT!
STOP THIS STORY AT ONCE!

"Why?" you ask. Well, don't you think it odd that a magic dragon should eat homework for lunch? Of course it is odd, for it never happened. It was a silly lie told to a teacher by a little girl named Sandy.

"This dragon stole my homework!" she exclaimed. "And he took it back and sat under a tree and ate it with ketchup and mustard. And that is why I don't have any to show you."

Sandy was unique. For she had an imagination as magical as Puff's smoke rings. Fantastic stories and songs would bubble from her brain, bounce from her mouth, and delight the world about her. Then something in Sandy's life changed. From that point on she told many foolish lies, all day long, to anyone, for any reason.

For instance, her father, on one of his weekend visits, asked her if she preferred a bicycle or a microscope for her birthday.

"Nothing like that," she answered. "I want to have you and Mom, both of you, take me to Mount Everest. Right to the top. They

9

have this special snow there that'll cure freckles."

Her father was baffled. "Sandy, you don't have any freckles."

"Sure I do, Dad. They're invisible."

Then, at home, when her mother asked if she'd washed the dishes as she'd promised, Sandy would usually say something like, "No, Mom. A great scientist just announced that washing dishes makes the germs grow. So if you want to stay healthy, you keep the dishes dirty."

And if she was playing baseball in the schoolyard, and missed three pitched balls, and the umpire called, "STRIKE THREE! YOU'RE OUT!" – she would argue, "Just because I have three strikes? Haven't you heard? Congress just passed this law. You get four strikes now."

Soon Sandy had lost all her friends. People simply don't like liars. All she had left was her big, shaggy dog, Muggs, who, full of innocent love and blind devotion, still believed every word his best friend said.

"A famous impresario," Sandy lied to Muggs, "said he was going to make me the star of the Russian Ballet!"

Muggs was delighted. He jumped up and licked her face, as if to congratulate the new ballerina. "Gee, Muggs," she giggled, "you believe anything I say, don't you?" The big, hairy dog nodded his big, hairy head in his big, hairy way that seemed to say, "Yes, my best friend, anything."

Sandy sprang up. "Want to chase your ball?"

Muggs, remembering the rules set down by Mom, shook his head no.

Sandy frowned. "I know Mom said we shouldn't play ball indoors. But...um...she changed her mind," lied Sandy. "So, FETCH!"

She tossed the ball, and it sailed halfway across the room, then smashed into her mother's favorite antique lamp, sending it crashing to the floor. And when her mother rushed into the room, Sandy cried out, "It was Muggs! I tried to stop him, but he jumped around and knocked down the lamp!"

Muggs was quite surprised to hear this version of what had happened. Although he didn't quite remember it this way, Sandy said it, so it must be true.

Sandy's mother came over to the sweet,

trusting animal. "I'm sorry, Muggs," she said gently. "You are just too big to keep in town. We'll have to give you back to Aunt Clara. She has a nice house in the country, and Sandy can see you in the summer." Then she turned and walked out to the hall closet to get his leash.

Muggs was most unhappy. He would miss his best friend very much. Sandy wanted to reassure him. But all she could think of was another dumb lie. "You wait and see," she promised. "I'm going to call in the Marines to get you back. You believe me, don't you?"

Yes, Muggs still believed her. He nodded his huge, shaggy head. Sandy hugged him close, and the fresh scent of the outdoors still clung to his coat and reminded her of all the good times they had together.

"Aw, you believe anything," she said, holding back the tears.

Her mother returned with Muggs' leash, slipped the collar over his head, and led him out to the station wagon. And when they had driven away, Sandy sat down glumly on the curb and rested her chin in her hands. If ever a little girl was all alone, it was Sandy.

She really needed a friend.

And far, far away, Puff the Magic Dragon felt her need. He quickly packed his satchel, hopped into the basket of his balloon, filled the gas bag with magic smoke, and, in an instant, was soaring high over Honah Lee, on his way to Sandy.

Both of them were in for a long, magic journey.

CHAPTER TWO

Sandy Makes
an Earthquake

Sandy sat alone on the curb for a long time, lost in her troubled thoughts. She was so preoccupied that she didn't notice the balloon with the dragon until it floated past her face. She sat up with a jolt. "HEY!" she shouted.

Puff stepped out of the basket and inquired, "I beg your pardon. Did you just see a dragon float by in a balloon?"

"Sure," said Sandy. "You."

"What a relief," sighed Puff. "For a moment I thought you were imagining me." He quickly deflated the balloon and tucked the gas bag into his pocket.

"Who are you?" asked Sandy uneasily.

"Oh, don't you remember me? My name is Puff. I'm the dragon who ate your homework. Delicious, too."

"But that was just a story. I made you up." Sandy was very annoyed. "If you're just one of my fibs I can make you go away. GO AWAY!"

Puff looked all around, then pinched himself to make sure he hadn't disappeared. "Am I still here?" he asked.

"Uh-huh," nodded Sandy.

"Then I suppose I am more than one of your fibs."

This was too much for Sandy. She got up and started toward the house. "I gotta go!" she announced. "I've got an important appointment with the Queen of France."

Puff was not impressed. "You have all the time in the world for appointments."

She turned back to him. "How do you know?"

The dragon reached into his pocket and took out his old alarm clock. He held it up and pressed two fingers down on the hands tightly. The ticking stopped. "I've stopped the clock 'twixt the tick and the tock," he explained. "We can go anywhere, do anything and, when we return, not one second will be lost."

"GO 'WAY!" shouted Sandy.

"NO WAY!" replied Puff.

"I'm warning you," said Sandy. "You'd

better run for it. Because...because..." Puff leaned forward with great interest. Sandy realized she'd have to make up a really good lie to fool him. She thought very hard and came up with a humdinger! "BECAUSE THERE'S AN EARTHQUAKE COMING! AND THE GROUND WILL JUST SWALLOW US UP!"

"If you say so," sighed Puff, puffing one of his magic, pink smoke rings.

Suddenly there was a rumbling so deep and powerful that Sandy could hear it in her chest and stomach as well as her ears. Then the ground under her feet began to dance to the awe-inspiring sound. "WHAT'S THIS?" she cried.

"Your earthquake, I assume," answered Puff. Then a crack appeared in the ground. It swiftly opened into a gaping hole. Puff took Sandy's hand, gently. "This way," he directed. And down they went!

Beyond the rainbow's time and space
Our friends are falling through
To a tunnel in a land beyond
The clouds of pink and blue.

They came down, finally, on some sort of barren wasteland. It wasn't a very attractive place, even for the bottom of an earthquake.

"Where are we?" asked Sandy.

"A long way from your home, I'm sure," said Puff.

"I don't want to go back there anyway," she announced.

Puff seemed surprised. "Why not?" he asked.

She couldn't really explain it, so she lied. "Because my house is broken, the pipes are squirting, and the electric wires are going 'Fizzzzz!' "

"Good gracious," said Puff. " 'Fizz-zzz,' you say?"

She didn't feel like elaborating this lie, so she changed the subject. "I wish I knew where we were."

Puff walked over to a rolled-up chart hanging from a pole stuck in the ground. "Perhaps this will clear things up," he said, and he pulled the chart down like a window shade.

"The Land of the Living Lies," said Sandy. "Sounds great. Where you don't have to tell the truth, and folks really appreciate a good lie."

The Land of The LIVING LIES

Where lies do go
when ye world
finds them out

Suddenly she heard a noise behind her. Startled, she turned around and gasped. Someone was standing not ten feet away, watching every move they made.

CHAPTER THREE

Exploring the Land of the Living Lies

It was a little boy. He watched Puff and Sandy quietly for a moment. Then his eyes widened, and he pointed to Puff with a trembling hand. "WOLF! WOLF! BEWARE OF THE WOLF!" he shouted, running away.

"What's wrong with him?" asked Sandy. "Can't he see you're a dragon?"

"Must be 'The Boy Who Cried Wolf,' "

explained Puff. "All the famous liars live here."

Presently, a tall, strange-looking fellow, with a long, spidery moustache, came down the rocky path. For a moment Sandy thought he was riding a horse. But then she saw he was wearing one of those cardboard play horses that clowns wear in the circus. His long skinny legs stuck out the bottom of the horse.

Puff recognized him immediately. "Just look who's coming to welcome us," he shuddered. "Baron Munchausen, himself."

"Who?" Sandy asked uneasily.

"Baron Munchausen," explained Puff. "The world's greatest liar. The most famous teller of tall tales who ever lived. Why, his lies have come down through the centuries."

The mysterious Baron slowly came closer and smiled coldly. "Welcome, fellow liars," he said, bowing low.

He seemed important, and Sandy thought she'd better make a good impression on him. "Seems like a wonderful place you have here, sir," she lied.

The Baron snarled cruelly. "HOW DARE YOU CALL IT WONDERFUL!"

"What's wrong with wonderful?" cried Sandy, cowering.

"IT IS AN INSULT!" screamed the Baron. "IN THIS LAND EVERYONE LIES! IF YOU SAY IT IS WONDERFUL, YOU MUST BELIEVE IT IS TERRIBLE!"

Sandy decided to change her story. "IT *IS* TERRIBLE! IT'S A TERRIBLE PLACE! AWFUL! YUCH!" And she made an ugly face to show just how bad it was.

The Baron smiled sweetly and petted his cardboard horse. "That's better," he cooed. "Enjoy your stay here. Feel free to wander hither and yon. The climate is beautiful. It never rains here."

Of course, that was a lie. For no sooner had the words oozed from Munchausen's lips than there was a bolt of lightning. The skies opened up, and rain began to pour down.

Sandy clutched Puff tightly. "Puff, I want to get out of here," she whispered.

"Why don't you just ask the Baron's permission and see what happens?" suggested Puff.

That seemed too easy to Sandy. Another lie was definitely called for. "He's the kind you have to trick," she explained. "Leave everything to me."

She turned to the Baron and called prettily, "Baron Munchausen. I'm a famous brain surgeon. And a king is very sick. And I'm the only one who can put a bandage on his brain. Otherwise it will mean war. So I have to leave. Okay?"

The Baron seemed pleased with the story she'd concocted. "You may leave any time you wish," he informed her with a slithery smile.

Sandy was so overjoyed she dropped her guard. "Really?" she hooted. "You mean that? NOW?"

The Baron held up his hand. "Now is not *any* time," he said firmly. "Now is a *specific* time. Find a time that is *not* specific, and you may be on your way." Then he laughed cruelly, pulled back on his reins, and galloped off, down the rocky path, his laughter echoing through the jagged hills.

"You've met the master," said Puff.

"Those were mean lies," sobbed Sandy. "He's awful."

"True," nodded Puff. "But remember, you tried to trick him first."

Sandy realized Puff was right. And suddenly she felt sorry. "Maybe, maybe I don't like lies as much as I thought I did."

Puff smiled. "Come on, let's see if we can't find a way out of this place." He took her hand, and they both started to walk along the rocky road.

As they traveled, they met more of the famous citizens of the Land of the Living Lies. There was the Purple Cow, that no one has ever seen; and the Pink Elephant, that some see too often; and, peering over a wooden fence, was a bald man with a long nose, the world-famous Kilroy, who always was there and never was anywhere.

These were a lot less terrifying than the Baron, and Sandy began to giggle. When they met the funny magician's rabbit who *seems* to, but never *does*, live in the hat, she burst right out laughing. Then she remembered her new feelings about lies, and she covered her mouth. "I shouldn't enjoy these guys," she said, "should I?"

"Why not?" asked Puff.

"Because they're just a bunch of silly lies."

"No, they are fanciful lies," said Puff. "And harmless fantasy is okay — and *fun!* I mean, *I'm* part fantasy."

Sandy was confused, but she really wanted to learn. "Aw, Puff," she asked, "how can I tell the difference between a real lie and a fantasy one?"

It was a difficult question. Puff thought about his reply, then replied thoughtfully. "A fanciful lie is hard to explain. It starts in your heart and bubbles to your brain. It wiggles your ears and away it goes. Then it comes right

back and tickles your toes. If it makes you feel
kind of song and dancy, it's more than a lie.
It's a wonderful fancy!"

Then, as if to illustrate, he blew a great big
smoke ring. And everything began to change
in the most fanciful way imaginable. For an
instant Puff became a birthday cake! And
Sandy became a tree! Then the sky became a
parachute! And to top that, the Earth became a
pea without a pod! Everything turned into
something wonderful and unexpected.

"WHAT IS ALL THIS?" cried Sandy with delight.

"Part of all the wonderment of what the world can be!" answered Puff, sucking back the smoke ring.

Sandy blinked her eyes, stunned. The magic was gone and they were back on the rocky path. And before she had a chance to reflect on Puff's magic, she looked up and saw that the clouds above them had formed themselves into words.

There was a message in the sky!

CHAPTER FOUR

Under Arrest

 The cloud message said:

PLEASE DON'T
EAT THE FLOWERS.
PLEASE DON'T
PICK THE APPLES.

But there was nothing but some stones on the ground. "I don't see any apples or flowers," said Sandy.

Suddenly one of the stones said, "I'm a flower! I'm a pretty petunia!"

"This is very confusing," said Sandy.

"Yes, it's just terrible!" said another stone. This one had the voice of a duchess. "Take me away from here. Pick me. Pick me, please," she implored.

Sandy felt sorry for her. "Aw, poor little thing," she said, reaching down and picking up the stone. "We'll take care of you."

Suddenly the duchess-stone screamed, "THIEF! THIEF! SHE'S PICKING THE APPLES!"

"But you're not an apple," cried Sandy. "You're a stone!"

Then the first stone began to bellow. "She's an apple! We petunias know apples from stones!"

"That's the silliest thing I ever heard!" snapped Sandy, annoyed now.

The stone who claimed to be a petunia looked up at her and screamed. "Ow! You're eating me! You're eating the flowers!"

"But I was just talking!" cried Sandy.

"HELP! POLICE! POLICE!" bellowed the duchess-stone.

Sandy heard a siren. Then a small motor-bike with a policeman on it came roaring down the rocky road. The policeman hopped off, and Sandy saw that he was just a little fellow with a rather familiar face. Oddly, he seemed to be made of wood! He clattered up to Puff and Sandy.

"AHA! PICKING APPLES! EATING FLOWERS, EH?" he piped. "You can't do that! You're under arrest!"

"How can you arrest us?" asked Sandy angrily. "You're just a little wooden boy. A marionette."

"NONSENSE!!" he screamed. "I AM A

POLICEMAN!" Suddenly, his nose grew about two feet longer, and branches came out of it.

Sandy gasped. "Puff, do you know who he is?"

"Pinocchio!" said the dragon. "Where else would he live?"

"This way!" screamed the policeman.

"SEND HER TO THE CAVERNS! TO THE CAVERNS!" cried the stones. "SEND THEM BOTH TO THE CAVERNS!"

The policeman escorted Puff and Sandy into a large cave-like room with a stone floor. At one end there was what appeared to be a prisoner's dock, made of stone. At the other end was a stone jury box and a judge's bench, also of stone.

"This looks like a courtroom," said Sandy. The policeman led them to the dock.

"I guess you're on trial," whispered Puff. He nodded to a door by the jury box. "Look, here comes the jury."

"All liars?" gasped Sandy.

"Oh yes," said Puff. First a pretty little girl in a party dress came through the door and took her place in the jury box. "She's the Social Lie," said Puff.

The little girl lied, "I'd love to come to your party, but I have a bad cold." And she gave a polite, artificial sneeze.

Then a long, skinny cowboy entered and drawled, "Back home we grow melons so big we can use the shells for swimming pools!"

"The Tall Tale," explained Puff.

Suddenly, a wild-eyed, bearded, little man, carrying a fish in one hand, pushed his way into the jury box and announced loudly, "BUBBLE GUM CURES WARTS!"

"The Meaningless Lie," said Puff. Then, noticing a fully dressed snake slithering in, he whispered to Sandy, "Next, the Vicious Lie."

The snake hissed. "Tommy wears T-shirts with torn tails-s-s-s. Pass it on. Hssssssss..."

Then Sandy heard the sound of mean and unkind laughter from above. She looked up and saw a gallery filled with all the liars in the Land of the Living Lies. A terrible lot.

"Puff, I'm scared," she whimpered.

Puff merely nodded in the direction of a huge, dark creature with a most unpleasant face. "Here comes the judge," he said quietly.

"GRABBLE SHLUB SLISH SNART," said the creature, climbing ponderously onto the judge's bench.

"The Monstrous Lie," explained Puff.

Then a small door in the judge's bench opened, and a tiny fellow with a bald head and a baby face skittered out and came right up to them. "Raise your left hand," he ordered.

"He's the bailiff," explained Puff. "A Bare-Faced Lie."

"Little girl," asked the bailiff, "do you promise not to tell the truth, the half-truth, and everything but the truth?"

Before Sandy could answer, the judge rumbled an order. "RAAAARZH! SCHPIV-ILY GORP!"

Suddenly, a gigantic fellow, dressed like a sideshow barker, came up to Sandy. He twitched his tiny moustache, glowered down at her, and snarled, "Isn't it true you zipped the zapper when you snipped the snoo?"

Sandy didn't understand one word of the question. "Who is he, Puff?"

"The prosecuting attorney," answered the dragon. "A genuine Flim-Flam."

The huge prosecutor started to dance as he continued with his cross-examination. "And furthermore, you frightened the flip by frying the frizbee! I put the case, that all the while the fluster flittered, your velocipede matriculated! DIDN'T YOU!!?" he roared.

"I-I don't know," cried Sandy, terrified.

"AHA! SHE ADMITS IT!" bellowed the prosecutor.

And all the spectators in the Gallery of Liars joined the judge and the jury as they looked down at her and chanted terribly, "GUILTY! GUILTY! GUILTY SANDY! GUILTY SANDY! GUILTY SANDY!"

Sandy had never been so frightened. She was so terrified she forgot everything she had learned from Puff and lied again. "NO, I DIDN'T DO IT!" she screamed. And, just as

she had blamed Muggs for breaking the lamp, she turned and pointed to Puff. "HE DID IT! HE CONFESSED! HE'S THE ONE WHO'S GUILTY!"

Luckily, dragons have stout hearts. For if they didn't, Puff's would have smashed into a thousand pieces. "Oh, Sandy, you can't mean that," he said quietly.

"YOU DID! YOU DID! YOU KNOW YOU DID!" she screamed, not daring to look him in the eyes.

And all the Lies chanted, "GUILTY DRAGON! GUILTY DRAGON! GUILTY DRAGON!"

The bailiff went out to the hall closet to get a leash. He came back and slipped the collar over Puff's head and led him off.

Would this be the end of Puff the Magic Dragon?

CHAPTER FIVE

The Truthquake

A dragon's magic lasts as long
As children's love is there
Puff's dragon eyes are filled with tears
Oh Sandy, show us you still care.

Puff sat in the center of the courtroom, the leash still hanging from his neck, and waited to be sentenced. Sandy came up to him.

"They said I could see you one last time."
Puff sighed. "Well, here I am."

There was so much Sandy wanted to say, but she couldn't seem to say the words that her heart was feeling. So, as usual, she lied. "You wait and see. I'm gonna call in the Marines to set you free!"

And, in the gallery, the Lies all chuckled appreciatively. Sandy looked up. Baron Munchausen leaned down from the mob and said, "Good lie, little girl. You're almost one of us now."

A chill went through her. She turned back

to Puff, desperately. "Do your magic and get us out of here! The way you did before, with the earthquake and all."

Puff gave a helpless little shrug. "I can't," he sighed. "My magic is gone until you tell the whole truth."

"Puff, I'm sorry," she said miserably. "And that's the truth."

Indeed it was, for it displeased the Gallery of Living Lies, and they started to grumble menacingly.

Puff put his paw to Sandy's lips. "Careful what you say, dear. You live here now."

"But I don't want to. I want to go home."

"Really?"

"Yes. But I can't. I told you about my house."

"Oh yes," said Puff, remembering. "It's all broken with squirting water pipes."

"It's not broken *that* way," said Sandy.

When the gallery heard that, they began to make most unpleasant moaning and groaning sounds. They seemed terribly unhappy.

Sandy looked up. "What's wrong with them?"

Puff smiled. "That was an important truth. And they don't like it at all. Finish what

43

you started to tell me. Please. How is your house broken?"

Again Sandy tried to make the words come. But the gallery had frightened her. She couldn't. She turned away.

"Sandy," said Puff, "if you don't tell me the truth now, this may be the last time I'll ever be able to see you. How is your house broken, child?"

"It's my folks," she said quietly. "Mom lives one place, and Dad another."

The gallery rose and screamed furiously, "STOP HER! STOP HER! STOP HER!"

Puff paid no attention to the mob. "Sandy, is it because of what happened to your mom and dad that you're telling these lies?"

"Yes. Lies are better than the truth, when the truth is . . . is . . . it was all my fault!"

The gallery relaxed and began to smile.

Puff frowned. "Little girl, you can't really believe that?"

"It's true!" cried Sandy. "I thought about it, and thought about it, and finally figured it out. *I caused it to happen!*"

With this, the gallery all stood up and cheered.

"What did I say? Why is the gallery so happy again?" asked Sandy.

"Because you just told a whopper!" snorted Puff.

"But I didn't lie to you!" she cried, all confused.

"Not to me, child. To yourself. You told the worst kind of lie there is. The Lie of Self-Deception! If you believe that, you'll be here forever!"

"But I did it!" she insisted. "My folks are all smashed up."

"They're not smashed," said Puff tenderly. "Broken people can't show love."

"Love?"

"They still love you, don't they, child?"

Sandy was startled by the question. She thought about it and then realized Puff was right. Her mom and dad did love her. She turned to the dragon. "And they *couldn't* love me if they were broken. And they *wouldn't* if I was the one who broke them. But they *do!* And that's the *truth!*"

The gallery, which had been growing more and more restless, now exploded with rage. They roared and stamped their feet and smashed their fists into the walls.

But down below it was as if Puff and Sandy didn't hear them at all. "And what *else* is the truth?" asked the dragon.

"The truth is it really wasn't my *fault!*" said Sandy, with wonder. "I feel so *good*, now!"

"ATTA GIRL!" croaked Puff, delighted. And the gallery thundered even louder. Great cracks began to appear in the walls. "Just say the words that you've got to say," sang Puff. "Just realize that you're really okay! And the walls come a-tumblin' down!"

"Puff, now I know what we came here for," sang Sandy. "And the walls come a-tumblin' down!"

Now small pieces of rock and stone began to break off the walls. The gallery began to collapse. Sandy looked up at the Lies and sang, "Just look at these lies that built that wall! I'll yell out the truth, and they're bound to fall!"

And they both sang out, "AND THE WALLS COME A-TUMBLIN' DOWN!"

CRASH! CRUNCH! BOOM! SMASH! SPLATTER!

As if to answer their song, the walls did indeed start to come a-tumblin' down. It seemed to be raining stones and lies of every shape and size.

"Another earthquake?" asked Puff happily.

"NOPE! A TRUTHQUAKE!" giggled Sandy.

"Wait a moment," said Puff, taking a deep breath. Then he blew a large, colorful smoke ring. "IT STILL WORKS!" he cried. "NOW JUMP!"

The two of them jumped through the magic smoke ring and were gone, as the rest of the Land of the Living Lies came crashing down. As far as Sandy was concerned, it was destroyed forever.

CHAPTER SIX

Home Again, and
That's the Truth

They found themselves on the curb again, in front of Sandy's house.

Sandy blinked her eyes. "Puff, what happened to the Land of the Living Lies?"

"The Truth set us free! Ta-da!" he said, doing a playful little dance. Then he took the old alarm clock from his pocket. "Now I must start time a-crankin' again. And you've got to get home."

"Will you still be here when time starts up again?" asked Sandy hopefully.

Puff smiled sadly. "No, Sandy. But you can think me up or write me down. And I certainly hope you do. There's no more need to waste that wonderful imagination of yours on a lot of silly lies."

"Thank you, Puff," said Sandy, "I'm going to miss you."

Puff nodded his head wistfully. "There will be other friends to take my place." Then he shook the clock. "And now — to start, alas, the magic clock. And move, once more, from tick to tock."

He gave the clock hands a nudge. The old timepiece began ticking loudly. And Puff was gone.

All was quiet for a second. Then Sandy heard a truly wonderful sound. Muggs' barking! She turned, and her great, hairy friend tumbled into her arms, licked her face, and plopped down in the exact same spot Puff had been sitting, just seconds before.

Puff made it happen, thought Sandy.

When Sandy's mother returned, she was quite worried. She really thought she'd lost Muggs when he jumped out of the station wagon. But Sandy rushed up to her. "Mom, Muggs found his way home! And, oh, Mom, he can stay, can't he? I told a lie before. Muggs didn't break the lamp. I did. And that's the truth!"

Telling the truth about a broken lamp may not seem like much, but to Sandy's mom it was like a miracle. "Thank you, Sandy," she said.

A little later Sandy's dad came over. He had a birthday present, which he handed to her. She ripped it opened and exclaimed, "Oh, Dad! My microscope!"

"It won't cure your invisible freckles," he said, and they both burst into laughter.

"That was just a silly lie," said Sandy, holding up her present. "This is what I really wanted."

And Sandy's dad shared the miracle.

She turned to Muggs. "You want to look for germs with my microscope?" Muggs nodded yes, eagerly. Then Sandy remembered. "Okay, but later. We made Mom a promise. Let's go do those dishes."

And after the dishes were done, and the microscope played with, and the pajamas put on, and the teeth brushed, and the covers tucked, and the door closed, Sandy slipped from her bed and tiptoed to her desk.

Remembering what Puff had told her, she picked up a pencil and began her first story:

"Once upon a time there was a magic dragon," she wrote, "and he just loved to eat homework with ketchup and mustard."

It was sure to become a classic.

SONGS

What the World Can Be

Words and music by Peter Yarrow

Medium tempo

(1) When a drag- on — be- comes a

birth-day cake, and a lit- tle girl a

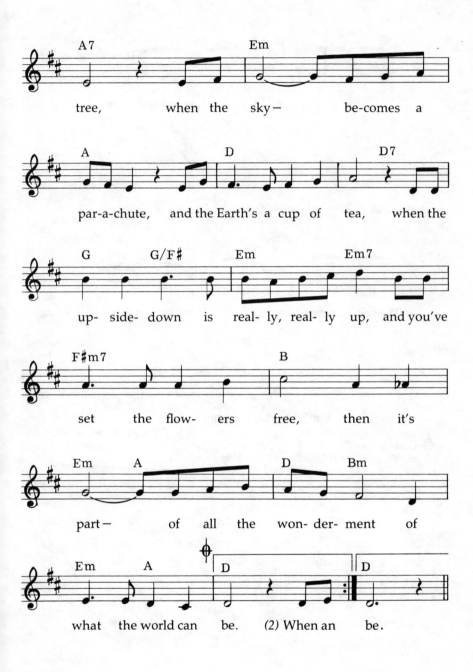

tree, when the sky — be-comes a par-a-chute, and the Earth's a cup of tea, when the up- side- down is real- ly, real- ly up, and you've set the flow- ers free, then it's part — of all the won- der- ment of what the world can be. (2) When an be.

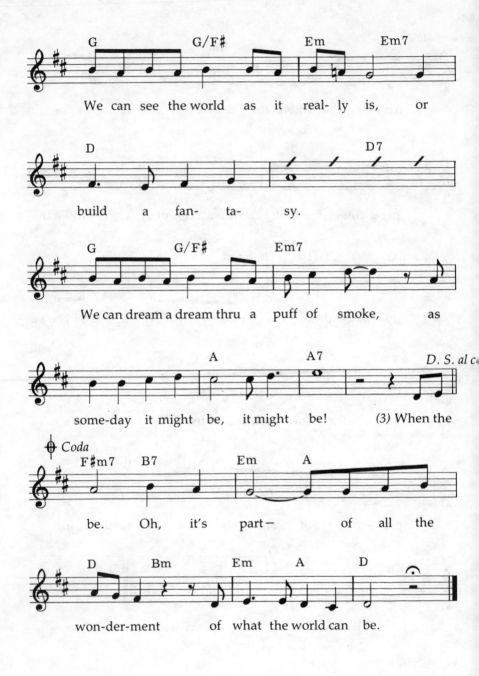

We can see the world as it real-ly is, or

build a fan-ta- sy.

We can dream a dream thru a puff of smoke, as

some-day it might be, it might be! (3) When the

D. S. al c

🎵 *Coda*

be. Oh, it's part — of all the

won-der-ment of what the world can be.

(2) When an ice-cream bar is a monument,
    and a glass holds all the sea,
    when the snowflake becomes a Jungle gym,
    and the moon's a tiny pea,
    when the inside out is really, really in,
    and the unicorn's set free,
    then it's part of all the wonderment
    of what the world can be.
    (to bridge)

(3) When the giant becomes a jellybean,
    and a sword turns into a snail,
    when a churchmouse becomes a chimpanzee,
    and a puddle turns into a pail,
    when the tippy-tippy top is at the bottom of it all,
    and the kites are all set free,
    then it's part of all the wonderment
    of what the world can be.
    (to coda)

The Walls
Come Tumblin' Down

Words and music by Peter Yarrow

Rubato

Just say the words that you've got to say, — and the

walls come a — tum- bl- in' down. —

Just re- al- ize that you're real-ly o- kay, — and the

walls come a—tum- bl- in' down. —   You
don't have to try —   to fool the world an- ymore, —   and the
walls come a— tum- bl- in' down. —
Puff, now I know what we came here for, —   and the
walls   come a— tum- bl- in' down. —
Sing out   the truth,   say what is real, —   and the
walls   come a—tum- bl- in' down. —   Now I

know how good that freedom feels, — and the

walls come a-tum-bl-in' down. — Just

look at those lies that built that wall, — and the

walls come a-tum-bl-in' down. — Just

yell out the truth and it's bound to fall, — and the

walls come a-tum-bl-in' down. —

"Lies are good, — you have noth-ing to fear, —" and the

walls come a— tum- bl- in' down. —   "You

don't scare me, 'cause I   don't be- long here," and the

walls come a — tum- bl- in' down. —

"Grib-ble shorb   yarg skleer," and the

walls come a— tum- bl- in' down. —

"Grib-ble your-self! We're leav- in'   here —"   and the

walls come a— tum- bl- in' down. —

Take off   your mask,   be who you are, –   and the

walls   come   a – tum- bl-   in' down. –

Dream your   dream, and   wish on   a   star,   and the

walls   come   a – tum- bl-   in' down. –